StoneSoup

Writing and art by kids, for kids

Editor's Note

A radio that thinks but cannot move or speak to help the humans around it. Mice who struggle with money and social acceptance. A dragon condemned to a harsh life.

This issue is a celebration of perspectives. Seeing from the point of view of an animal or an object, or even from the vantage point of a very unique person (as in "Rainbow") reminds us of how limited our own perspective is, in the larger scheme. It also reminds us to treat others—people, animals, and things—with kindness and respect. Their lives may be different from ours, but they are still valuable.

This issue is also a celebration of winter and the holidays. Every year, I hope for snow in December, and the past few years, it hasn't always happened. Maybe our idea of winter and our image of the holidays will need to evolve as our climate continues to change. In the meantime, let's hope for snow!

Finally, in this longer-than-normal issue you'll also find an excerpt from *Born on the First of Two* by Anya Geist, whose book I selected to publish as an editor's pick in our 2020 Book Contest. I'm thrilled to announce that, as of December 1st, you can order Anya's book at our store—stonesoupstore.com! Anya's novel follows Maya as she journeys from the Land of the Clouds down to Earth, where she was born, and where she is convinced her destiny lies. Anya's book gripped me from start to finish. It's the perfect book to curl up on the sofa with on a cold, cold wet day.

Wishing you the best this holiday season,

On the cover:
Winter Wonderland
(iPhone 8)
Elodie Weinzierl, 11
Waban, MA

Stone Soup (ISSN 0094 579X) is published eleven times per year—monthly, with a combined July/August summer issue.

Thirty-five percent of our subscription price is tax-deductible. Make a donation at Stonesoup.com/donate, and support us by choosing Children's Art Foundation as your Amazon Smile charity.

To request the braille edition of *Stone Soup* from the National Library of Congress, call +1 800-424-8567. To request access to the audio edition via the National Federation of the Blind's NFB-NEWSLINE®, call +1 866-504-7300, or visit Nfbnewsline.org.

StoneSoup Contents

ART

POETRY

Beauty Among Ancient Walls
(iPhone 6s, iOS photo filters)
Peri Gordon, 11
Sherman Oaks, CA

The Lonely Radio

A radio grapples with its essentially passive existence as the world crumbles around it

By Avital Sagan, 12
Ithaca, NY

Radios have become old-fashioned. I know that through the snippets of conversation I hear as I sit on my table. Despite that, they've never done more than talk about replacing me.

There's a man who uses me the most often. He has an impressive mustache and is often referred to as "the Communicator" by the people who talk through me.

I connect people who are far away. It may not be the most exciting job—I care very little about human politics—but it's fulfilling to know what I'm doing is helping people.

And when people aren't using me, I can look out at the island of Floracion. My room is near the top of a skyscraper that towers over the rest of the city. There are impressively tall buildings and people constantly going about their business, but that's not the best part. The best part is the flowers.

Floracion is overrun with moonflowers, aptly called "gigantics," white flowers that only bloom at night and sometimes grow over a dozen feet wide. People make room for them everywhere. On the sides of buildings, in storefronts, on roofs.

Most people are awake during the night to see the flowers, and I can't blame them. It's spectacular.

And the Communicator comes into my room every day. He, like me, has an important job. He has to stay awake during the day to communicate with nearby cities and countries. Like me, he's made a sacrifice—for me, my mobility, for him, his sleep schedule—but we're both improving Floracion. Together.

He uses me to talk to other people while I listen, learning what I can and speculating about the outside world. Those conversations make my life, stagnant as it is, worth it.

I'm proud of what I do. It's an important job, and Floracion is—in my highly biased opinion—one of the best cities in the world. How could any sterile buildings match the flowers' beauty? The way the city makes every hour of the night busy?

At some time in the evening, the Communicator leaves. His assistants sometimes stay longer, even sleeping here in some extreme cases, but they eventually go too. And I'm alone.

But one day, he doesn't come.

It's not his absence that worries me, but the fact that he said nothing.

I watch in horror as the city comes alive, but not in the usual way.

His assistants are also gone. They always discuss their plans where I can hear them.

Where are you? I think. Static bursts from my speakers for a moment, but it's gone as soon as it starts, and I get no answer.

I look down on the island. It's night, yet no one is out. That's beyond unusual. Not a single car is driving on the streets, and if there are any people, it's too dark to see. Most of the lights on the buildings are out.

I check the radio stations, but there's nothing but music and static.

Even the flowers seem different. With no sounds from vehicles or the usual racket from people, the white petals that almost shine in the moonlight seem eerie. They're more like the pressed flowers that used to be kept in the room. Beautiful, but dead.

There's no wind. Not a single leaf on any of the flowers moves, but one moonflower—a gigantic that must be twenty feet across—moves.

It rotates its head, the movement slow and deliberate. This is not the wind. It's a predator looking for prey.

It's not doing that on its own, I think, but the irony is not lost on me. A sentient radio thinking that the flower cannot do anything on its own.

Perhaps the world is stranger than I know.

And like a flipped switch, there are suddenly more. The gigantics closer to the ground are moving to face the street.

I remember one of the Communicator's assistants mentioning a plant called the Venus flytrap. They have thin hairs that, if brushed against by an insect, will cause them to snap shut.

The moonflowers are hunting.

I watch in horror as the city comes alive, but not in the usual way. The flowers look everywhere, sometimes leaning down or looking up.

One of them looks at the mountain. It has no eyes, but the way it keeps staring makes me feel like a hapless fly, my doom about to be sealed. I wouldn't have been surprised if the moonflower grew legs and started walking toward me.

But it didn't, and I'm grateful for that.

In the unknown time I have been around, I have perfected the art of zoning out. Of letting time pass by me as I blank, making unbearably long nights no more than a dull minute. I employ this tactic now, tuning in to one of the music stations for good measure.

I think they call this genre "jazz." It washes over me, helping me relax despite the strangeness of my situation. I don't get much about humans, but I understand why they love music so much. It's almost magical.

Then the elevator bings.

I'm reconsidering my moonflowers-growing-feet theory when someone decidedly human steps into the room.

It's a boy. He's much younger than even the youngest of the Communicator's assistants, a small girl with gravity-defying curls who had seemed to prefer looking at dog pictures than helping.

When he looks at me, I remember why I do this. He looks at me like I'm his last hope.

But more than that, he's scared. *Terrified*. Tears hover in front of his eyes, balancing carefully on his lower eyelids without falling out.

Does he know what's going on out there? I wonder. He must, given how upset he seems. It was creepy enough for me to see the flowers moving. For someone who might be just feet away from them—that would be beyond frightening.

The boy rushes toward me and begins to fiddle with me.

"Please," he says, the tears finally beginning to slip down his face. "You have to work. You have to. I can't die here."

I feel bad for him. My ability to manipulate the world around me, to do anything more than change the channel, is limited. But I can help him in small ways.

I adjust my inner workings, setting myself to a channel that the Communicator often used. He'd talk to a man he called "sir" and "mister." There was always a level of deference to this man that the Communicator never gave to anyone else. The man had to help this boy.

"Hello?" the boy says. "Can anyone hear me?"

A female voice responds from the other end. "Yes. I'm Carmen. Who is this?"

The boy smiles, wiping away some tears with his sleeve. "My name is Daniel. I'm in Floracion. I need help."

Carmen doesn't respond for a moment. "I'm sorry, but this is meant as a private channel. You should call the police if you need help."

"Wait!" Daniel yells, his voice echoing around the small room. I hear a slight gasp on the other end. "Please. The police aren't answering. People are going insane, and they're trying to get me to smell the moonflowers—they say it'll make me feel better. I don't know what's going on."

His voice begins to crack as he continues. I'm sure that this will be the end of his troubles. Carmen will send as much help as she can give and get him off the island.

But the moment I think I know what a human will do, they prove me wrong.

"This is not meant for pranks. I advise you to go back home." Carmen's tone has gone from cordial to steely. "Goodbye."

"No!" But Daniel is too late. She's gone.

I expect him to start sobbing again, but another look has appeared on Daniel's face: horror.

He tries to talk again but seems to choke on his own words.

"You can't," he whispers. "I can't die here."

I feel bad for him, but I'm soon distracted by the familiar bing from the elevator.

But this time, instead of relief, I feel an inexplicable worry. Daniel's eyes widen slightly. "Is someone there?" he calls.

Hide, I try to yell, but my speakers can only release static. *You're not safe here.*

Footsteps come closer, but something is wrong. It doesn't sound like a human. It doesn't walk; it drags. And the noise I hear—that's nothing that a human would make.

A whining. Like a hurt animal.

Once, the Communicator played a horror movie on his tablet. My view of it from over his shoulder wasn't the best, but I was scared nonetheless. For several nights after it, I had trouble blanking out like I usually did. I kept imagining monsters in the dark and doors that shouldn't be opened but always are.

Now I'm in the movie.

The door to the room opens, revealing a woman in a dirty summer dress with dark hair and soft features that remind me of Daniel's, although I've never been one to distinguish humans well.

But that look in her eyes, the dead look like something inside her is rotten—that's impossible to miss.

And Daniel sees it too.

I almost miss the pot in her hands. Two moonflowers are growing in it, both of a decent size, but nowhere near the size the flowers can sometimes reach.

"Don't do this, Mom," Daniel pleads. "This isn't you. You don't have to do this."

I wish his words meant anything, but the woman doesn't respond. She stumbles forward, making that same whining noise.

Daniel pushes her back, and she loses her grip on the pot. It falls to the ground and shatters.

His mother stares at the pot's remains. Her whining gets louder as she lifts the flowers with all the solemnity of a pallbearer carrying a coffin.

Daniel tries to rush past her, but she slams into him as I watch helplessly. She shoves the moonflowers under his nose. He tries to resist, but after a moment he goes limp.

They stay like that, mother hunched over son, for a few minutes. A solitary tear runs down her cheek as she stares at him—some remnant of the human she once was.

After a little while, she drags him out. I think I see Daniel's eyes flutter open, but then they turn into the hall and I'm left wondering what he's about to do.

So I wait.

I hear the elevator ding for the final time that night. Everything is silent save for the jazz station I listen to again, trying to forget my fears in the tune.

And like the nights after I peered at that horror movie, I can't blank out. All I can do is watch as a city falls below me.

But even as my world crumbles, as I feel devastation on a level I've never experienced before, as I try to scream with a mouth I don't have, the jazz keeps playing. On and on.

I don't know how to die. All I know how to do is play music that has become more grating than soothing. But I don't have the energy to change the channel. I don't have the energy to change my fate.

Through the days and nights I keep waiting for an end, but I don't find it. I watch planes fly and flowers burn, but the finale I seek never comes.

The music has looped so many times, I know every note by heart.

I resign myself to the fact that my death will only—if ever—come when Floracion is burned to the ground or reclaimed by the sea.

And no one noticed the lonely radio, watching the city from above. It wished for nothing but a way to finish its miserable story, yet it knew that long after the words stopped it would still be waiting for its life to end.

Two Poems

By Gideon Rose, 9
Dallas, TX

Cold Heart

This man has little food,
Little water,
Has not eaten in two days,
Only thinks of love.
Once a person, or unhuman I should say,
Punches the poor man and throws his supplies in the trash.
The man gets on his knees for mercy
And still only thinks of one thing:
Love.
You may think this story is crazy.
It's not.
Because that man was me.

Old Man

Once an old man stepped to me
We sat down on the chair
He said to
remember
this day
But now that I see that man
was no other than
Nature

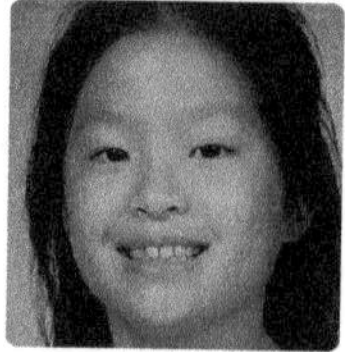

Silent Snow (Acrylic)
Yutia Li, 11
Houston, TX

Rain, Rain, Go Away

An outdoor field trip goes ahead as planned, despite the torrential downpour

By Yanling Lin, 10
Falls Church, VA

The rain was pounding down hard as I tried to seek shelter under the small makeshift ceiling of umbrellas. My shoes and pant cuffs were soaked, but the water continued pouring without any sign of stopping. Shivering in the cold, I had gone off my gears. My brain started wandering, wondering if this misery would ever end. I wanted to be home with a cup of hot cocoa, reading a book. However, I did not have that choice, and instead, I was in this soaking mess. Clearly, this field trip had not gone as planned.

It was 2016, and my school was on a school-wide field trip to a broad field where we could play many games and hike. Today, it was also supposed to be sunny.

As I woke up that morning, I could hear the sound of the rain relentlessly hitting the ceiling with a sound that imitated a river. I wondered, *Are we still going on the school-wide field trip, or will it be canceled from the rain?* The latter was the better choice, but the school principal seemed not to agree.

As the morning progressed, the rain did not soften, nor stay the same; the weather decided to make the sky pour oceanfuls of water down to the ground. When I arrived at school, I was hoping and praying the trip would be delayed a week or two, or canceled. As I heard the rumors, though, my hopes sank further and further to the ground.

When the overhead speakers started sounding for the classes to start filing into the busses, that confirmed my hypothesis, and all hopes of an okay day faded to dust. Hearing the constant squeak of shoes against the tile floor, I sat stone-faced in anguish. On the outside, I still had my slight grin, frizzy hair, and composed arms. On the inside, I was a total wreck.

What are we going to do? Are we going to stay on the bus until the sun comes out? Make a pit stop and come back (my secret hope), *or endure the hardships of a rainstorm outside?* Thoughts swirled through my mind.

"Ms. Kim's class, please enter your assigned bus," I heard over the speakers.

My nightmare became a reality as I started walking down the hall in a single-file line and sat down on the slightly moist bus seats. The air smelled wretched—of spoiled milk and rotten eggs, and there were even food wrappers and stains everywhere. I heaved a massive sigh as I tried to get as comfortable as humanly possible on the grossest bus in the country. I sat with friends, which was the only thing that made the ride even somewhat bearable. Somehow, I was able to forget the scene I was in and laugh—but just a bit, as when I inhaled again, I was reminded that I was not in my classroom, not even on an average bus.

"I wonder how this trip will go. I mean, it's still pouring outside, and this trip is supposed to be in the fields. Are we going to stay on the bus?" I said to my friend.

"I know, right?! They tell us we're going to do so many cool things outside, but then it starts raining!"

"I just hope we can go back to school where there's a roof above my head."

"Me too."

Soon, the bus jolted to a stop. *Oh, noooooooo . . . !* the little voice in my mind groaned as the long stop meant we had arrived, and being outside in the severe rain was next. The storm had not calmed even a bit, and I knew going out would not be pleasurable at this point.

I stepped out of the bus feeling as if I were flowing down a river with a high current. Raindrops the size of my fist were coming down in bucketfuls, and the asphalt below me was engulfed in a few inches of water.

My group and I huddled underneath the umbrella the chaperone brought, but alas, it was designed to protect only one person, so many of us got wet, including me. We continued walking and simultaneously getting soaked by the falling water, and soon got to the grass. I thought it couldn't get worse, but walking on the grass proved me wrong. Every time I stepped, the wet and mushy grass squished under me, giving me the feeling of stepping in an icky slime. With the rain, all the dirt had turned into mud and was surrounding my foot with every step.

Soon, the mud-water started seeping into my shoes, soaking my socks, and making me feel even more uncomfortable. Even though I was wearing my winter jacket in April instead of December, I felt colder than I'd ever been in my life. I suspected it had something to do with being drenched head to toe by the second, it being only about 40 degrees outside. I overheard some teachers talking in the background, and I hoped with all my heart that it was about going back to school. As I continued eavesdropping, though, it became clear that I would not be going anywhere for a while.

I was shivering under a crowd of umbrellas brought by chaperones. I wondered when we'd get back to the school building. Today, we'd planned to play field games like cornhole and horseshoes, and even go on a hike. These fun activities had all been canceled.

I was now thoroughly engulfed; it looked like I had just taken a dip in the pool. I stood waiting extremely impatiently, hoping my ordeal would be over soon. But as the storm adamantly continued, I slowly started to accept the situation. Before, I had been perplexed, and only felt angry that I was still out here and sad that I couldn't go back. Now, no matter how stubborn I was, I realized I was not in control, and I could either deal with it or deal with it. It wasn't easy to do, but as my only option, I did just that.

Approximately thirty minutes later, we started walking back toward the buses. *Wait a minute. We're going back? And we came to do nothing just to go back? How pointless!* I ranted in my mind. Even though I was slightly annoyed that we had come here just to get drenched and go back to school, I was still ecstatic that I would be leaving this miserable place. I sat with my friends once again, ranting and venting with each other about how horrible the field trip had ended up being. I wasn't nearly as upset anymore.

When I got back to school, I was slightly less wet, but not much. My hair looked slicked back from the water, but not in a nice-looking way. My shirt was mostly wet, except for the top half of the torso. My pants were soaked, especially at the cuffs from constantly grazing the grass. My shoes and socks had become the wettest of all during the trip. Luckily, I had a change of clothes that I had brought with me that morning in case of disaster, and a disaster had certainly happened. I changed into fresh, dry clothes, and the rest of the day went peacefully.

When I got back home, I learned that my brother had still had to go on the hike in the pouring rain, and at that moment, I felt lucky for my circumstances.

Cedar Tree

By Eva Worsick, 9
St. George's, Bermuda

Cedar tree growing tall,
I remember when you were small.
I climbed on your branches but didn't fall.
Some rope and wood should make something good.
It should.
When swinging from your branches,
I feel like I have wings.
When I tell you my secrets,
you never say a thing.
The Christmas tree orbs they swing, they swing, they swing.
And they look like the sun,
brightening up everything.

Bridge in the Snow (Fujifilm X-T1)
Claire Lu, 13
Portola Valley, CA

Two Poems

By Analise Braddock, 9
Katonah, NY

Parallel Christmas

Parallel lines don't stop.
Christmas doesn't stop.

The snow sticks and not a light flicks out.
Not a curve or a bend in a parallel line.

The time ticks and tocks for Santa.
Comes and goes for Christmas, but the lines of Santa's are forever.

Get ready, hang the stockings.
Set out the cookies and milk.
Light up the tree for a parallel Christmas.

The Revolutionary War

The muskets
The words
The guns

The roses wilting to the battle
That would not be likely be beat

The soldiers' cold faces
Molded by fear and braveness
Outdoing each other

No more trapped by England
No more being told what to do
Time to be free

Guarding the Garden (Watercolor)
Audrey Champness, 12
Green Cove Springs, FL

Street Cats

Lorraine gets fed up when the cats in her neighborhood won't stop following her around

By Annabelle Vaughan, 9
Gibraltar, UK

Cats never stopped following Lorraine in the street. They even followed her to the park, on holiday, also to school. Lorraine got fed up, so every day she went in disguise, but the cats got super scared when they could not see her.

One year ago, Lorraine saved a cat from being run over. The saved cat told all the other cats to follow her to feel safe.

Lorraine lived in a small town called Berry Bay. She had lived there for two years. Lorraine was sad in Berry Bay because she'd had to leave all her friends behind in Midtown. She had been sad ever since.

She had her own cat called Jerry that did make her happy. One day, Jerry let all the cats in the house and all the cats saw her getting ready in her disguise, so now the cats still followed her. People laughed and stared, so Lorraine got so, so fed up she said, "You cats go away or I will call animal control!" She really loved animals and felt bad but did not know what else to do. The cats sadly went out of the house. Even Jerry left.

They went under a box. It started to rain. The cats were wet, but the cats did not care because they were so sad their hearts had flown off. The cats did not feel safe anymore, but the cats did not give up hope.

When Lorraine was asleep, all the cats went under her bed. The next day Lorraine felt bad. She got a bag of cat food and looked all around the town, but there was not a cat in sight. All the cats were still under her bed. Every day, Lorraine left cat food outside her house. The cats started to realize Lorraine still loved them, so they ate the food, and Lorraine saw that they were eating.

Lorraine's mum said she was thinking of going back to Midtown because she did not like seeing her so sad and there was a new job in Midtown.

The cats heard and were trying to think how to keep Lorraine in Berry Bay. They were thinking of ways to make Lorraine's mum happy so that she would not want to move again, back to Midtown. Jerry said, "We need all the street cats to set a meeting." All the street cats came. They said they would make Lorraine stay.

"So," Jerry said. "How can we make Lorraine's mum the happiest lady in

Even Lorraine's mum started to miss Jerry, because Grump turned out to be a destructive dog.

the world? Tom, what do you think?"

Tom said, "We have to put fish in her mum's bed."

"Good, Tom. You will get a fish too," said Jerry.

So the next day the cats put fish in Lorraine's mum's bed. The mum was so mad, she grounded Lorraine for a month.

The cats met again and came up with a new plan. Jerry said, "This will make her happier than ever!"

Then the cats made her mum breakfast: bad milk, cat food rolls, and mice. The mum got so, so mad she locked Lorraine in her room for another month. Lorraine saw all the cats under her bed. She hugged Jerry but said to all the street cats, "IT WAS YOU! DO YOU EVEN KNOW WHAT YOU DID? YOU LOCKED ME IN MY ROOM FOR A MONTH." She called animal control, but they did not come. She hugged Jerry, but all the other cats went sadly away.

They went under a bench, and Tim said, "You should give up on her."

But Bill said, "No, we need to know if she still cares."

The next day her mum went and got a bulldog for Lorraine because she thought it might make her happy. She was so happy the bulldog did not like cats.

"Where is the cat?" said the bulldog.

The cats were in the airport. They had small bags, and one of them had a suitcase that used to belong to Lorraine's dolls.

Lorraine was having fun naming the bulldog. Lorraine said, "Hmm . . . I will name you Grump."

Later, Lorraine was sad in her room. She missed Jerry, who had been missing since Grump arrived, but she did not want to say it.

Over the next few weeks, things got worse and worse. Even Lorraine's mum started to miss Jerry, because Grump turned out to be a destructive dog. First, he tore open Lorraine's favorite dolls, chewed her homework, and got mud all over her carpet. But then, one night Grump got into the fridge; ate lots of greasy, slimy chicken; spilled blueberry smoothies on the rug; ripped open packs of rice, honey, and her mum's special oatmeal breakfast; and with sticky paws made tracks through the whole house and ended by snuggling into Lorraine's mum's bed. So Lorraine was woken up with, "WHAT HAPPENED! GRUMP! GRRRRRUUUUMP! LORRAINE!"

It took Lorraine all morning just to clean the kitchen floor. When she saw the rugs, she started to cry.

Miles away, waiting to stow away on their flight to Cape Cod, where they had heard the buildings and streets were all made out of fish, Jerry felt a sudden flash and heard Lorraine's voice in his head saying, *Please help! Come back, Jerry.*

Lorraine's mum packed up Grump in the car and took him back to his old owner, and Lorraine felt so sad she hid under her covers. A little later, when she woke up, at first she thought her mum was angry, shouting from downstairs, but then she realized she was shouting, "Oh Lorraine, how did you do it? This is amazing! Lorraine, it's wonderful."

When Lorraine ran downstairs, she could not believe her eyes—everything was sparkling clean, the rugs were perfect, her mum's sheets hung to dry in the garden bright white, where there were also lots of cats sitting in the shape of a heart. The fridge was also full of fresh food: cheese, chicken, chocolate, yogurts, and fizzy drinks. All of Lorraine and her mum's favorite things. Jerry was sitting in his favorite chair in the living room, curled up with a smile.

"I still think she would have liked that tuna I found in the airport bins," Tim said to Bill.

"People are strange," Bill said.

"I love you all," Lorraine said. She was stroking them in the garden, where she had filled lots of boxes and crates with warm pillows and sheets and put out bowls full of fish, cat food, and milk. But she could not find any mice!

The Acorn (Samsung Galaxy S9+)
Joey Vasaturo, 10
Colebrook, CT

Ma's Riches

A poor mouse family prepares for a visit from their king and queen

By Fiona Clare Altschuler, 11
Parkton, MD

Corn Lily and Day Lily lived several miles from an abundant wood. They were twin mice, and their family was very poor. They lived in a small burrow, poorly furnished, on dry, cracked ground. Their mother planted little seeds every year, but the plants died before they were knee-high to a splinter. Their father walked for many hours beneath the blazing sun to gather nuts where the grass was lush and the trees tall and fruitful. But he was often exhausted by the time he got there, and never had enough time or strength to pick enough acorns and hazelnuts for his family. Day Lily and Corn Lily worked very hard, but still they were never properly fed or clothed.

They might have moved to richer ground if it were not for one thing. Day Lily was very quiet and sickly, and one of her hind legs was crooked, and she walked with a limp. She couldn't walk all that far, and a journey to suitable land would take a day at the very least. Although thin and light, she was much too heavy to carry for hours on end. Corn Lily was different. She was strong and outgoing, and a great help to her parents.

"Oh, Ma," Day Lily said tremulously one day, while sewing a shabby apron for Corn Lily.

"Yes, my darling Day Lily?" Ma said quietly, catching sight of her daughter's face.

"If it weren't for me, we might have moved to richer ground. It's because of me we're so poor," the little mouse whispered, tears in her soft brown eyes. "But I'm just a burden. Just a b-burden!"

"Oh, you aren't a burden. Look at your sewing. And you cook and knit wonderfully. You aren't a burden. Don't cry, child."

Suddenly Corn Lily ran in.

"Ma, Ma!" she cried in excitement. "King Straw, Queen Birch, and little Prince Barberry are coming! They are stopping at every mouse's house, and that includes us!"

"Good rivers!" Ma gasped.

"Oh, Corn Lily!" Day Lily shouted, leaping up and grabbing her sister's paws.

Just then, Da slipped into the little burrow. "What's all the noise?" he asked.

"Slope, the king, queen, and prince are coming!" Ma told him breathlessly.

Then the little mouse peered past the jewels and fine silk and studied the king, queen, and prince's faces. They didn't look happy, she realized.

"Oh, Poppy!" Da said. He smiled in amazement, and then his smile faded slowly.

"Da, what's wrong?" Day Lily asked.

"Oh, they'll scorn us," he sighed. "The royal family is proud. And they'll scorn us for being poor."

"Oh, Da, they wouldn't scorn someone who works so hard!" Day Lily cried, flinging her arms around Da's neck.

"Or someone who's so nice like you, Da," Corn Lily shouted.

"I don't believe anyone in the world has such wonderful daughters," Da said.

Three days later, there was a brisk knock on the door. Corn Lily opened the door and gasped, giving a hasty bow. Day Lily looked up from her knitting and scrambled to her feet.

"H-hello—I mean, Your Majesty," Corn Lily stuttered.

"Please, d-do come in." Day Lily said, self-consciously aware that every mouse was staring at her crooked leg. "I-I'll go get Ma. W-wait here, please."

She hobbled as fast as she could to Ma's room.

"What's wrong, child?" Ma asked.

"Oh, Ma, they're here! King Straw and Queen Birch and Prince Barberry, Ma!" Day Lily said.

"Great rushing rivers!" Ma said breathlessly, running to the door and smoothing her fur.

King Straw came in first, looking sniffily around at the humble burrow and the shabby mice who lived in it. Queen Birch followed, fussing over Prince Barberry, who just kept goggling at Day Lily's crooked leg. She felt herself getting hotter and hotter. The rich robes the royal family wore were fringed with rubies and emeralds. Queen Birch's paws shone with rings, and a golden crown lay on King Straw's head. Corn Lily was amazed by their fine garments, and self-consciously glanced down at her plain, russet gown. Then the little mouse peered past the jewels and fine silk and studied the king, queen, and prince's faces. They didn't look happy, she realized. The queen's ears drooped, the king's eyes were dark with gloom, and the prince's brow was wrinkled in a sulky frown. She wondered how they could be so sad when they were so rich.

"Sit down, Your Majesty." Ma said, flustered.

They didn't sit.

"Where's your husband?" King Straw asked importantly.

"Away, sire, gathering acorns. Hazelnuts too," Ma answered, nervous at the seriousness in the king's tone.

"Surely acorns wouldn't grow here?" the queen said. Somehow, the surprise in her tone made Corn Lily angry. The queen knew no acorns grew here. She had asked it just out of spite!

"No, my lady. He walks many hours to gather them," Ma murmured.

"He works hard?"

"Oh, Sire," Day Lily said suddenly. "Da works very hard. Very hard indeed."

"You say he works hard," King Straw said snidely. "But then why are you so very poor?"

Ma stood a little taller. "Oh, Sire, I have to say I'm much, much richer than you are."

"You are, are you?" The king smiled, but it wasn't a nice smile. It was a smirk, and it made Corn Lily even angrier.

Prince Barberry giggled, pointed at Ma, and whispered something in the queen's ear. Corn Lily clenched her paws tight.

"Yes," Ma answered. "I am. But not in money, Sire. In joy. My daughters and my husband and the beauty of the sunset bring me so much joy that I am richer than you—hundreds of times richer. Oh, yes, Sire. Hundreds of times richer. If joy were money, this house would be so full we wouldn't have room to get in. If joy were money, it would overflow this shabby burrow and fill the world. And so I am much, much richer than you are. Riches do not buy happiness, Sire."

King Straw was speechless. He struggled for a retort, then, looking angry and embarrassed, swept Queen Birch and Prince Barberry away. As they left, the prince was still staring at Day Lily, but for once, she didn't mind.

When they were gone, Day Lily and Corn Lily leapt onto Ma, hugging her fiercely and feeling richer than the richest king.

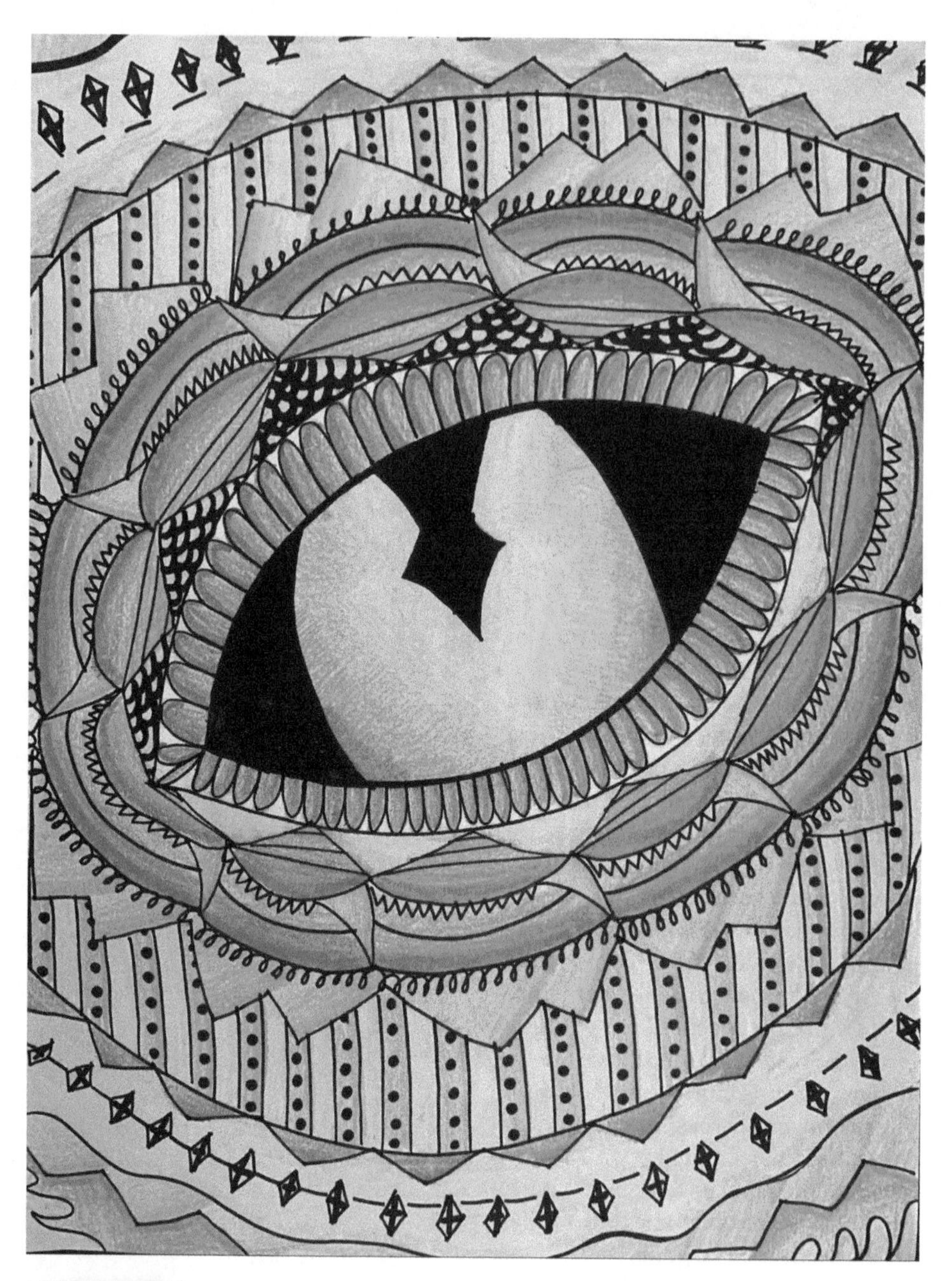

Dragon Eye (Pen and colored pencil)
Maggie McGoldrick, 9
Yardley, PA

Blink

Being a guard dragon means a lonely and difficult life

By Lucia Osborn-Stocker, 12
Browns Valley, CA

I paced, on high alert, by the doorway, the rusty metal chain around my neck clunking. I growled at a rider passing by. My dark-green scales felt clogged with dirt, the spikes along my back chipped and dented. The huge castle doors behind me loomed angrily. My stomach hurt from hunger. Though my food dish still had some chunks of fresh meat, I would save those for another day. I was patient.

That was something I had learned from my time as a guard dragon. When you work for humans, you tend to learn things. You *have* to learn things, and be smart, and strong, or you don't survive. You are disposable. You might succumb to the harsh weather—the stifling heat of the summer, flies buzzing around your ears, or the freezing cold of the winter, snow forming drifts, and stringing icicles along your sharp spines. Or maybe the humans would find a replacement, slaughter you, and use your thick, scaly hide for armor.

Another thing I learned was how to tell when someone meant trouble. The key was to read the energy around them. Some troublemakers slink in the shadows. Those are the rare kind, and the most dangerous. Those are the ones who try to sneak past the castle walls. Most humans, however, aren't that ambitious. They're satisfied just throwing food and laughing. I never complained. Sometimes the food-throwers saved my life, though they didn't know it. I saved their projectiles for when the hunger was too much to bear.

Today, some of these troublemakers, the food-throwers, were loitering by a market stall a few feet away. They were scruffy, probably street kids. Their clothes were in muddy tatters, their hair reminding me of a robin's nest I saw several months back.

The bird had laid three light-blue eggs. Then I watched as the hatchlings grew, strengthened by the unwavering care of their parents. Then one day they were gone. The little fledglings flew away, spreading their wings on the wind and soaring out of sight. I never saw them again. But the next year, the mother returned and used the same nest as before.

I watched the street kids. They inched closer. I snorted a small flame.

The kids recognized the sign. That was another thing that I had learned: when someone wanted a fight or just needed a warning. The kids backed away. I lifted my snout to the sky. The sun was setting, the clouds turning vibrant reds and pinks and purples. One or two stars were beginning to shimmer against the dark blue abyss of the sky. The humans began trickling back to their homes. I curled up on the stone ground. I had learned long ago that it was useless trying to get comfortable. The nightmares still came.

As I was beginning to fall into a fitful sleep, I heard a noise. It sounded like the padding of small paws. Squinting one eye open, I saw a young fox pup coming my way. She was scruffy, her bushy tail bedraggled and her fur matted. Ribs showed through her dusty pelt. She was too young to survive the night without a mother.

I pretended to be asleep. I heard her creep closer, and then she quickly snatched a hunk of meat from my food dish. She glanced at me, my large pointed teeth, sharp spines along my back. I opened my yellow eyes just enough, and blinked slowly. The fox tilted her head, pricking her pointed ears. Then she curled up into a tight ball, and fell asleep. I noticed she was shivering. I paused, unsure. Finally I draped one scaly wing over the ball of fuzz. The fox yipped in her sleep.

For the first time in my long life, I slept without nightmares.

Pieces of Sunset

By Sage Millen, 12
Vancouver, British Columbia, Canada

Daylight fades, unravels,
revealing intertwining coils of color.
Dusky lavenders to emerald greens creep through the sky
like enchanted vines on an old brick wall.
Colors flicker and dance,
candle flames lighting up the heavens.
Fierce oranges and hot pinks explode like dragon fire,
flooding the world with color for a mere second before
the colors shatter, sending pieces of sunset everywhere.
Catch one.
It's mesmerizing, but I look up
just in time to see that
everything has ended in stars.

Above and Below (Watercolor)
Saylor Creswell, 8
New York, NY

Let It Be

The writer learns a valuable lesson after bringing home a pet worm

By Billie Brown, 12
New York, NY

As I crawled through the lush grass, I could hear the cardinals singing a happy morning song and smell that fresh cut-grass smell that people have tried to bottle but never succeeded. I took a deep inhale to try and consume as much as I could, but ultimately it triggered my hay fever, which made me sneeze loudly. I had recently taken a liking to sneezing as boisterously as I could to scare my family. As I opened my eyes in recovery, I observed something slimy, wiggly, and tan-colored slithering in the soil.

"What's that? I said inquisitively.

As I leaned in closer, my friend Annabelle screamed, "It's a worm!" even louder than my sneeze.

Now that would normally gross out the average child and prompt them to scuttle away, but I'd recently realized my life's potential was to be a jungle explorer, following a family trip to Costa Rica. There I'd had my first taste of termites and lost my heart to a baby sloth. So, I now fancied myself the next Steve Irwin (I was born in Australia after all), and this was as close as I was going to get to the jungle in a Long Island backyard. Surely this miniscule creature needed protecting from the perils of the suburban Northeast. I needed to save this annelid from imminent threat, before a ravenous hawk or vicious adult foot ended my rescue mission prematurely.

This wouldn't be my first foray into animal rescue. I had been practicing taking care of stuffed animals at home for over five years by this point, running an animal rescue center out of my bedroom. I hadn't lost a patient yet; a few had lost a limb or an eye, but they were all alive and well (in the bottom of my closet somewhere). I had been accumulating quite the exotic world animal collection over these years, with a kiwi bird from New Zealand, a polar bear from France (an impromptu gift from an airport shop from my Dad), an echidna from Australia, a British bulldog, and a mouse from Orlando, Florida. Surely, I was ready for the big time now. It was time to rescue my first *wild* animal.

As I approached the worm, I played out the rescue mission in my head: *As you can see, the human female is approaching the mysterious creature here in the suburban jungle,* I said to myself in the voice of Sir David Attenborough (after all, I am half British). *This appears to be a critter of the common earthworm variety.*

"Hurry up, Billie!" My friend Annabelle interrupted my musings. "I need to pee!"

I snapped out of my head and back into my body. I began to creep up on the worm from behind so that I wouldn't startle it and miss my chance. *Easy does it. Just a few more steps . . .*

"Worms don't have eyes, Billie!" said Annabelle obnoxiously.

I didn't think she was enjoying this game as much as me, and before I could stop her, she pinched the worm between her thumb and index fingers and pulled it out of the ground. I watched it stretch till its head (or tail, who can really tell), sprang back out of the ground. It wiggled in one last attempt at freedom, but ultimately the stronger species triumphed. She dropped the worm into my hand. It tickled as I cupped it with my other hand and carried it toward the house.

It was time for phase two of the operation: convince my parents to let me keep him as a pet. (I now know that earthworms have both male and female organs, but at this point I'd decided he was a boy.) Annabelle had now ditched me to trade Pokémon cards with my brother, so it was on me to deliver from here.

As I approached the kitchen, I could detect the comforting scent of hot tomato soup bubbling on the stove, combined with the buttery aroma of grilled cheese sizzling on the skillet. My mouth started to salivate, and I almost forgot about what I was there to do, but a wiggle in my hand brought me back to the task. And what better time to present Mom with a worm on my filthy hands than when we're about to eat?

"Mom, can I please keep this worm that I found in the backyard?" I said.

"Billie, I think worms are meant to stay in the wild, in their natural habitat," she answered back. "And go wash those grubby hands!"

I wasn't about to give up that easily, "But he is going to get eaten out there, Mom!" I said gloomily.

"That's just part of nature's life cycle," Mom said very practically, as she often did. But I didn't want the worm to get eaten—he was now my friend.

"Just one night. Pleeeeease!" I begged.

"Fine. One night only, and then tomorrow you set it free!" She never could bear my whining for too long.

"Okay. Thanks, Mommy," I said merrily. So, I had kind of accomplished phase two. I might not get to keep him as a pet, but at least he could have a sleepover.

I carried him back outside to find some things in the backyard that would work to make him a home. I grabbed twigs, leaves, rocks, and on a final impulse, some flowers to brighten the aesthetic. Personally, I find brown on brown a little depressing, even for a worm.

Later that night as the worm and I settled down, I sang one verse of "Rockabye Baby" to Worm, as I'd named him, and promptly fell asleep. Jungle exploration had proven to be a tiring business! I had sweet dreams about the fun Worm and I were going to have the next day.

I came to the realization that the only thing that the worm needed rescuing from that day was me.

The next morning, I woke up to the sun filtering through my eyelids. I peeled the covers off, anticipating seeing Worm playing in his new home. Much to my horror, I realized he wasn't there. I poked around the twigs to see if he was hiding underneath, but I couldn't see him anywhere! I pulled everything out of drawers, lifted carpets, looked under my bed, to no avail. I started to panic, thinking that he had run away because he didn't like me, or maybe he had crawled into my ear while I was asleep and was now living in my body. *What have I done? Now he is lost, and I will never be able to find him.*

I decided that I should look in his enclosure one more time just to make sure he wasn't there. I moved around all the rocks and twigs. I was starting to lose hope. Finally, in the corner of my eye, I spotted the familiar ringed pattern of his body, right up in the corner. As I squinted to get a closer look, to my confusion, I noticed there was not one, but two worms. Quickly, my hopes that the worm was actually a girl and had given birth overnight were shattered. The two worms were in fact the two halves of the original worm's delicate little body that had dried up and split in half overnight. In that moment my heart shattered as easily as his fragile little body had from a night of central heating.

After a breakfast of pushing my food around my plate because my stomach felt like I'd swallowed a rock, and the humiliation of the "I told you so's" I had to endure from my parents, I decided I needed some personal closure. I buried Worm that morning, less than twenty-four hours after we'd met, in a private ceremony. It was a short but moving memorial in which I laid him to rest in the soil I should have just let him be in in the first place. I shed a few tears and promised Worm that I would never take a wild animal from its natural habitat again. It may have only been twenty-four hours, but I felt like I'd matured a few years in that one day. I realized that love and care alone wouldn't be enough if I didn't also understand the needs of the animals I wanted to help. I came to the realization that the only thing that the worm needed rescuing from that day was me.

In the years that have passed since, I've focused less on "hands-on" research. I have continued learning about animal needs from doing research in books and online, visiting rescue centers, and observing them in their natural habitat instead of trying to bring them into mine. My knowledge grows every year, along with my collection of stuffed wild animal toys. My hope is one day I can include this mini memoir as part of my own full memoir when I achieve my (still current) dream of rescuing animals. I will dedicate that memoir to Worm (2014–2014), who was able to help me vow that from that day forward, I would truly help and never harm another animal again. His life won't have been in vain, and I aim to help infinitely more animals than I ever harm.

A Beautiful Wood

By Sean Tenzin O'Connor, 5
Bishop, CA

Beautiful Wood:
In the light of the lamp
Many rocks
Sitting aside
Resting in place

In the dark
The shadows cast
Lights and lamps
Throughout the night

Hanging down
Towards the book
The poems written
With many hooks

Worms slithering on the piece
An earthquake it seems
With many trees

Mountains and Rain and Rivers of
Color
Throughout
The piece of wood

Many slopes
With curved flat ends
At the bottom. It may seem that it’s not cold.
A Chord of Pine Trees in the Night.

Peacock (Pen)
Sophia Zhang, 8
Hinsdale, IL

The Peacock

An unexpected visitor alights on the writer's roof

By Jack Moody, 10
Richmond, VA

It just stood there, like it was supposed to be there. It might be in Asia, but not at our little white house in Henrico County, Virginia. There was a peacock on our roof. That's right, a peacock. My sister, mom, and I were standing on the deck leading into my parents' bedroom, morning air slapping our faces. We were watching a peacock strut on our roof, its face facing the yard.

"How did it even get up there?" I asked no one in particular. *How did it even get up there, seriously?*

But the way it was strutting could give you a thought that it owned the house, the street, even the county! Maybe even the country! And it was dressed like it too. Even though it wasn't showing off its assortment of beautiful rainbow tail feathers, it had a sea-blue body and a large patch of green on its neck, right under a beautiful light-blue eye.

It soon started calling to something in the yard. I looked into the yard to find another peacock disappearing into the trees! The other peacock looked exactly like the peacock on our roof.

The peacock soon flew off our roof, and the spectacle was over.

I went back into my room to get ready for school. If there is one thing I learned about peacocks from that dazzling event, it's that they have a place everywhere, even in America, the place where you least expect a peacock to be.

The Attack of the Christmas Lights (Phone SE)
Eliana Pacillo, 12
Walpole, MA

Rainbow

Brianna's head is in the clouds, and she's happy that way until a comment from her art teacher pushes her to change

By Lindsay Gao, 9
Dublin, Ohio

What are rainbows? People think rainbows are those colorful arched things that fade quickly. Why? Rainbows aren't always arches. They can be all shapes and sizes. I can see rainbows anytime, everywhere. Whether it's sunny, cloudy, or snowy, I can see them. Looking at rainbows, being able to decipher them in the atmosphere, is a thing that is very special to me.

"Brianna!"

I get jerked out of my thoughts by mom's voice. It's a sunny afternoon. I was lying on my back, staring up at the sky, as usual.

"We are having dinner in twenty minutes."

I shook my head, focusing my attention on answering my mom's voice. "What is it?"

"Chicken and broccoli."

"Can't we have pizza and ice cream sundaes?"

"No!"

I slumped, groaning. The rainbow in the sky shifted into an image of two slices of pizza, their cheese melted and gooey. Next to it was a chocolate-and-vanilla ice cream sundae with a rosy red cherry on top. I moaned. I really couldn't believe it.

"Stop it!" I cried.

The rainbow morphed into Winnie the Pooh flicking honey at me.

"Ugh! You're making me even hungrier!"

The rainbow morphed into a smiley face.

Grumbling, I laid my head on the bristly grass. My rainbow persisted. It turned into two puppy dog eyes. I sighed, but slowly my face morphed into a smile. I couldn't help it. I laughed. No one could make me laugh, except my rainbow. My rainbow understood me and actually made me happy. I wished anyone else did.

None of the kids at school really accepted who I was, and I couldn't imagine being friends with even one of them. I remembered the whispers and snickers that followed me like a swarm of angry wasps. Kids avoided me like the plague, and I had no friends whatsoever. Then there were the teachers. They looked so concerned about me and worried about my grades. I could see the disappointment they kept carefully hidden in their eyes. And parents. My mom scolded me, saying stuff like,

She said I should draw a normal rainbow. Maybe she was also implying that she wanted me to be normal.

"You need to get your head out of the clouds. Stop your mutterings about rainbows. You need to get serious, Brianna." Other parents, though, were worse. They sent me hostile glances at pick-up and pulled their children close when they saw me pass.

Suddenly, a mosquito buzzed past my face. The sun was starting to go down, I realized, and jumped up. "See you tomorrow!" I called up to the rainbow as I raced back inside my house.

The next day, our art teacher clasped her hands together excitedly. "We will be having an art show featuring rainbows."

I couldn't believe this was actually happening! I pulled out my rainbow sketchbook immediately, flipping through the pages until I found my favorite one. It was a cute face with a banana mouth, two cherry eyes, and a giant letter "Q" in the middle like a nose. This rainbow shape I chose was strange, but in my opinion, also beautiful. I admired it for a second. Then I started to color the background blue, with fluffy white clouds, and a small quarter of the sun.

Filled with excitement, I turned in my drawing after class and eagerly waited for approval. "Is it good?" I asked anxiously. I watched as her eyebrows furrowed. My art teacher was my absolute role model. I adored her. She always understood me. I was sure that she would understand my drawing too. Great minds think alike, right?

"It's . . . interesting," she finally said. I could see her trying to muster a smile. Finally she managed a thin one.

"Oh," I said. "Well, thanks." I started to walk toward the door.

"Oh, and Brianna?" she called after me, her eyes sincere. "Try to draw an actual rainbow next time."

I ran out the door as fast as I could. All of the students, the other teachers, the parents, they shunned me, and I didn't care. But my art teacher was the one who understood me the most, the one who should know me the best, and I heard her back there. She said I should draw a normal rainbow. Maybe she was also implying that she wanted me to be normal. I felt so lost, like a traveler without a guide. My heart remained loyal to my rainbow, but my brain insisted on listening to my art teacher. *Listen to her*, my brain whispered. *She is a professional.* Finally, my brain won.

A few days later, after a big rainstorm, I ran outside with my rainbow sketchbook, just like before. I sat down on the still-wet pavement and started to draw the standard rainbow. I messed it up several times, my tears staining the pages. I felt like someone was suffocating me with all these rules. But I persisted. I needed to do this. Finally I got the lines shaped perfectly, and the colors in confinement. The rainbow above me lowered down and nudged me. I covered my eyes. It kept nudging me.

"Stop it!" I screamed. "Leave me alone! You only give me misfortune."

As if showing my determination, I ripped out all the previous drawings of my rainbow and crumpled them one by one. Then I ran inside, closing the curtains. I would begin my life fresh and new again, starting with the rule of rainbows.

The new version of my drawing was so appreciated by everyone that it made its way to the art show on the conference night. That night, as I stood in front of it, I felt the admiring looks of other students. I am quite popular among them now.

"I am so proud of her improvement in school. She never has daydreams anymore, and she gets straight As." My teacher came out into the hallway with my mom. They kept on talking as more parents and teachers walked past smiling at me. I smiled back.

But then my attention was drawn to the drawing again. I didn't know why I felt so strange. I just did. Ever since I had drawn it, my rainbow had disappeared. I missed it so much. No matter what I told myself, I couldn't resist it. I knew I had to make my rainbow come back. So, I took my drawing home that night. I had to make some changes.

The next day, I again stood in front of my artwork. Under the arch of the rainbow, there was the Eiffel Tower and the Statue of Liberty; there were also dragons, unicorns, dogs, and cats, and even some pizzas and ice creams. All of these tiny pictures sparked memories, flowing so freely that I could barely believe it. The snapshots of these days spent with my rainbow flooded my mind to the brim. All of these shapes didn't clash with the rainbow arch. Instead, they made a rich harmony. The standard rainbow wrapped around the other pictures in a warm hug, embracing them. And they in turn filled the arch with colorful lights that showed brightly, making the artwork complete.

A crowd of younger students surrounded me and my drawing, whispering about what they thought it was. I turned around and confidently told them: "It's my rainbow."

Serenity

By Nora Cohen, 11
South Jordan, UT

On my porch
Seeing white
Falling from grey clouds
I walk away
From the
It's peaceful
And serene
The mountains
Are beautiful
Taking a deep breath
I walk away
From the snow

Distinction (iPhone XS Max)
Aiyla Syed, 13
Asbury, NJ

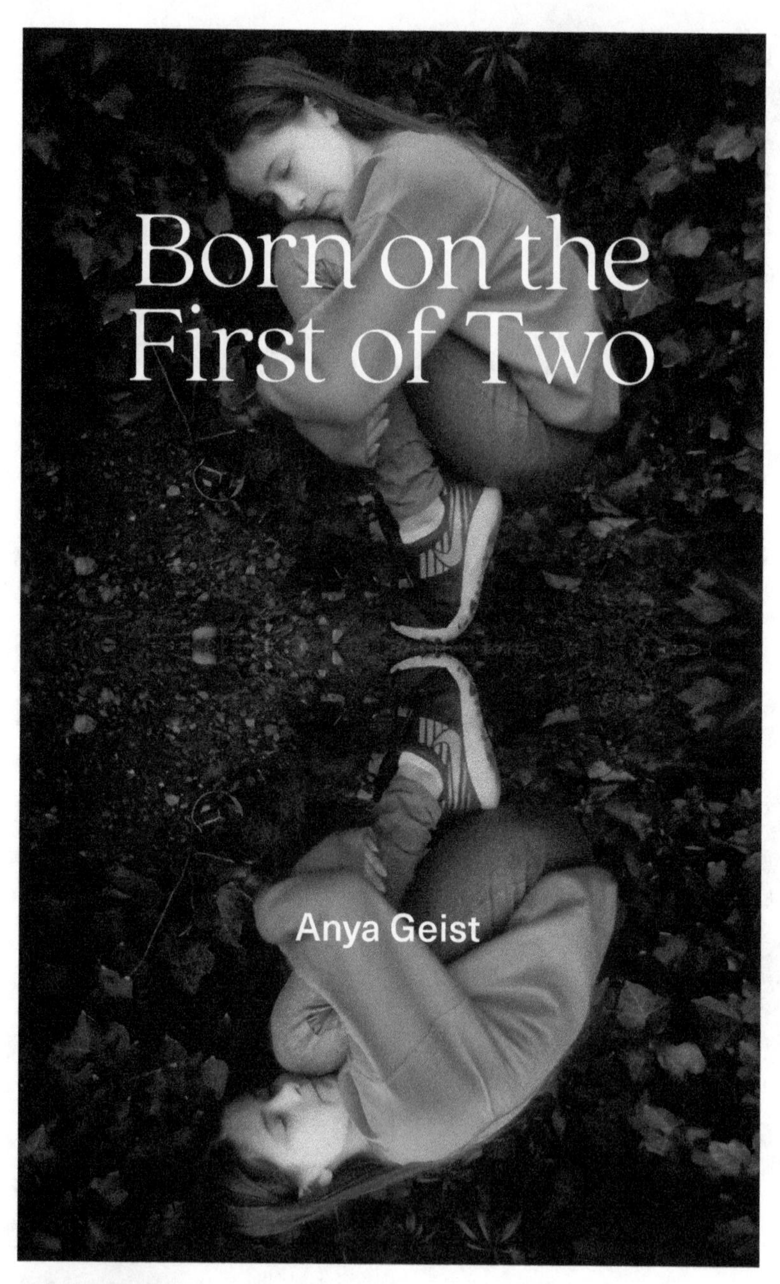

Book cover:
Enchanted (Canon SX600, Snapseed, Adobe Photoshop)
Sage Millen, 13
Vancouver, British Columbia, Canada

An excerpt from Born on the First of Two

Editor's Choice in our 2020 book contest

By Anya Geist, 14
Worcester, MA

Born on the First of Two was released on December 1, 2021.

You can order the book at Amazon or Barnes & Noble, and at our store: **stonesoupstore.com**

Prologue

Inhale, exhale. Inhale, exhale. The girl's breathing was labored and fast, the way it always was when she had this dream, this memory. It was a strange dream; it seemed to linger in her mind, tickling its edges like light in her peripheral vision. She'd had it for as long as she could remember, but she never became quite used to it; every time it came to her in her sleep, she found herself unsettled.

The sky was light blue, and the sun radiated its warmth down on the Earth. Birds chirped contentedly in verdant, leafy trees while bees hummed along as they flew from flower to flower, careful not to damage the soft, delicate petals.

The girl—then just a baby—sat on the ground just beyond the shadow of a small cottage, running her hands through the cool, glossy grass. She laughed at its touch, the way it slid along her chubby palm, and gazed up at the sky in wonder at the occasional fluffy cloud that drifted through on the mercy of the breeze, sweet air pumping its way into her lungs. She wanted to go up there. She wanted to be in that dazzling blue and run her hands along the clouds. She giggled merrily at this gorgeous day.

Here, the dream-memory became fragmented, shattered visions stabbing her mind.

The sky became dark, dominated by threatening clouds that seemed to reach up into space and cast jagged shadows over the June day. The birds stopped singing, and the temperature dropped.

She could feel the warm air leaving her lungs, cold, thick air forcing its way down her throat instead. It was searing, like a block of ice. She gasped for breath, rasping and wheezing, unable to cry as numbness spread through her, jamming into her arms and legs.

Two blurred figures appeared. One—she realized it was her mother—ran toward her, unclasped a golden necklace from her neck, and fastened it around the baby's neck. "You'll know how to find us," the woman whispered hoarsely.

The girl/baby, for now she was not sure which one she was, held out her hand, but her mother was already racing toward the gate in the white picket fence, rejoining her father.

"Stay back!" they called at the clouds. "Stop!" Their voices rang with fear and shook with weakness.

Now, outside the fence, there were many dark figures cloaked in dark robes that matched the army of clouds above. Their voices were deep and rumbling, like thunder that was mad, thunder on a rampage.

"No!" the girl's parents shouted. "Stay away!" But the figures were advancing, opening the gate, and the coldness was tightening its grip and the wind was howling.

Then her father turned to the sky, tears in his eyes. "Save her!" he yelled. His voice echoed into the sky.

And suddenly the air twisted like vines wrapping around a tree, and the girl was falling up, sucked into a dark tunnel. The coldness vanished, replaced instead by a constricting feeling as the air and darkness seemed to tighten—for it was as if they were one thing—and the girl was left writhing, shouting into emptiness as she tried to fall back to Earth to see her parents one last time.

She awoke. Her sheets were twisted and her chest tight, as if there were cords binding it. She sat up in bed, panting, and clutched her neck, grabbing the golden necklace that had been placed on her so many years ago. She wrapped her fist around it, feeling the cool metal soak into her sweaty hand, and tried to relax, staring into the rich darkness of her room, so different from that of the tunnel. She knew it would be a long time before she allowed the waves of sleep to crash over her once again.

Chapter One: **Stars Up and Down**

"Maya!" Auntie's voice flowed like honey, rich and deep, through the little house.

"What?" By contrast, Maya's voice was sharp and clear, like water.

"It's suppertime." Auntie stood at the foot of the stairs, shouting up to her niece's room.

"But I'm busy, Auntie," Maya complained. Auntie could hear her sigh.

"Maya, in the eleven years you have lived in this house, you have never once skipped supper, and I do not intend for you to start now." Auntie's tone should have told Maya that this was nonnegotiable.

However, Maya either didn't pick up on this, or ignored it. "But I have homework!"

"You can do your homework after supper!"

In her room, sitting on her bed, Maya jutted out her jaw. "Do I have to?"

"Yes. Now I'll be out on the porch. Get your supper and come out there." Auntie's receding footsteps told Maya she was going outside.

Begrudgingly, Maya slid off her bed, lay on the floor for a good ten seconds just out of spite, then picked herself up and began storming down the hallway and downstairs. She wasn't mad, per se, just highly annoyed. However, it is always more fun to storm downstairs than to walk.

She picked up a plate of spaghetti in the kitchen and headed out onto the porch, sitting down with the air of someone who is being forced to do so. "Are you happy now?" She glared at Auntie.

Auntie sighed placidly and swirled her spaghetti around with her fork. "Maya, I'm always happy when you're with me."

Maya's hard, emerald-green eyes, flecked with silver and gold, softened for a moment before she resumed her pretense of anger. "Hmph." She stabbed a meatball on top of her spaghetti. Her thoughts blew around crazily as she tried to find a way to fuel the fire of her own annoyance. As she settled on the perfect method, her eyes lit up slightly, the green becoming more alive, a wild forest.

Before she had a chance to speak, though, Auntie interjected: "Maya, why are you avoiding my eyes?"

"I'm not," Maya answered, all too guiltily, her eyes wandering to a spot just over Auntie's ear. "You know," she began, preparing to launch her dagger of anger into Auntie's heart, "my p—"

"Maya." Auntie's voice was firm now, not concerned, but curious. "Why aren't you looking at me?"

Instead of answering this time, Maya just went ahead and launched her attack. "My parents would have let me do my homework and miss supper." Her voice was laced with poison.

Auntie did not look provoked, though. She merely shook her head sadly. "Maya, don't go there. It's not fair."

"Not fair to you, maybe," Maya exclaimed, now truly angry without knowing why. "Because you know I'm right!"

"No—" Auntie tried to say, her blue eyes swimming.

"Have you ever thought that maybe it's hard for me to not have parents, huh? Have you ever thought that it's weird living with someone I call my aunt, someone I'm not even related to?" Darkness was setting around them, though the porch remained illuminated. The stars were beginning to come out, and the night air was cool and sweet.

Maya's eyes shone with tears, but still she avoided Auntie's gaze. She fingered the golden necklace around her neck. A thin pendant hung from the chain, and as Maya traced her fingers over the engraving of a dove, it grew warm to her touch.

"Maya," Auntie pleaded. "Look at me."

"No."

"Maya, please. You don't want this anger. It doesn't deserve you. You are better than it."

"I—"

"We both know that you get caught up in your anger very quickly. But you don't have to. Look at me."

"I don't want you to use your power," Maya spat out. They both knew what that meant. Auntie's power was to calm people down, the way others could teleport or fly.

Maya hated the way it felt when Auntie used her power, the way it seemed to submerge her in a garden of sweet-smelling flowers. The way it forced the anger out of her, whether she wanted to keep it or not. It didn't matter whether her anger was justified or not—Maya wanted to be the one to send it away, not to have it overpowered by perfume.

Auntie stared at the table. "Okay. You need to calm down, though."

"I know," Maya admitted. She could feel her anger slipping away from her, vanishing through the cracks in the porch.

"Look." Auntie tilted her head. "Look out past the porch. The night is so beautiful. The stars are too." Her face adopted a serene glaze as she looked off into the darkness.

"The stars are always beautiful," Maya muttered, her anger rallying one last time. Still, she stood up, her chair scraping the wooden porch, and rested her elbows on the porch railing. The wind swept her dark brown hair over her shoulder, stroking it like a parent she couldn't have.

"I wonder what it's like down on Earth," she mused. "I wonder if they look up at the clouds and wish they could be up here with us." She recalled having had that very thought in her dream. How strange it was that she had been brought up to the Land of the Clouds immediately after desiring that very thing.

Auntie came to stand with Maya. Together they looked out into the darkness, at other homes, at the towns of the Land perched delicately on the tops of clouds. "It's beautiful there," Auntie sighed, recalling her adventures on Earth. She looked down, where a gap in the clouds revealed tiny orange lights—human life. There were stars up and down.

"Though not many people ever get to see it."

Maya kept her mouth firmly shut, knowing that this last sentence was directed at her, a sort of "don't even think about it until you're old enough." In her mind, however, she was already travelling to Earth. What would it be like to see the stars from down there?

Chapter Two:
The OCT

The next morning dawned bright and clear. The sun had just come up when Maya awoke to her alarm. She turned it off and rose from bed, shaking sleep from her eyes. Pink-golden light spilled into her room, coating her desk and bureau, bed and bookshelf. She pushed the window open and let the sunlight hit her face, relishing its warmth in the frigid morning air.

She dressed in a simple tunic and cloak, then proceeded to go downstairs for breakfast. The smell of scrambled eggs caused her stomach to grumble. Auntie was setting two pieces of toast on plates, her silver hair neatly plaited, as Maya sat down at the kitchen table. As there was no precipitation above the clouds, they ate supper on the porch almost every evening, after the sun had warmed the wooden floor. But in the morning, it was still too cold to sit outside.

"Good morning," Auntie said. Her tone was welcoming and warm, like an embrace, but Maya sensed a note of hesitancy. Neither of them had forgotten their fight from the night before.

"Morning," Maya replied, greedily grabbing a plate of toast and nearly shoving it down her throat. It crunched pleasantly in her mouth. "Where are we today?" Maya inquired through a mouthful of toast.

This was not an odd question in the least. In fact, most children asked it every morning and evening as well. Since the "land" of the Land was clouds, they often moved from place to place—wherever the wind blew them—every day. It was an exciting game for little children who loved trying to guess the correct answer, and an interesting bit of trivia for everyone else.

"We're over southern France this morning," Auntie informed Maya. "So it should be warmer today."

"Good," Maya said. She supposed weather could be cold on Earth, but it could be absolutely freezing in the Land—frigid to the point where you had to wear three heavy layers.

Maya finished her breakfast and bid farewell to Auntie as she grabbed her backpack and headed out the door, wrapping her cloak around herself.

She skipped along the sidewalk, careful to stay away from the precipice at the edge of the cloud. People did occasionally fall off. Some could fly back up. Maya had no idea what happened to the others.

"Hey!" a voice called from near Maya. She whirled around and saw her friend, Scarlett Clayden, leaving her house, her two little sisters in tow.

"Hi, Scarlett," Maya yelled back, walking toward her friend. "What's up?"

"Nothing, really. I have to take my sisters to daycare this morning because Mom's on an assignment."

"Oooh." Maya's eyes sparkled in the sunlight.

"Yeah. I don't know much about it, but if you wait for me in the park while I drop these two off, we can walk to school together and I'll tell you."

"Sounds good. See you there."

Maya started off again. As she left her neighborhood, with all of its houses in neat rows, she began to see more and more people. Some biked in the streets, some walked, and some flew. And Maya knew there were many more commuters who were teleporting.

She reached the park, with its towering trees, and sat down on a bench. The ways of the Land were unknown to most people. In school, they learned about Earth and its people, but they never really talked about why the Land worked the way it did. As far as Maya was concerned, no one knew how trees could grow above the clouds, or how the citizens of the Land could survive, and even thrive in, cold temperatures that could kill a human. The Land of the Clouds was a mystery, and Maya was fine with that.

She was just pulling out some homework about the geography of Earth when Scarlett strode up to her. "Hello," Maya said, looking up at her friend.

"Hey." Scarlett sat down on the bench next to Maya and peered over at the homework Maya had out. "It's plateau: P-L-A-T-E-A-U, not 'plato.'"

"Oh, right." Maya grinned sheepishly. "Wait, what did you get for question four? 'Liquid precipitation on Earth?'"

"Rain."

"Okay, same." She stood, and they began to walk. "So, the assignment?"

The two girls were obsessed with Scarlett's mother's assignments. She was part of a select group allowed to visit Earth in order to make sure that the world was running smoothly, that no human was in danger of messing it all up. Maya and Scarlett got up from the bench and walked through the lovely green park as Scarlett told Maya all that she knew.

"Mom didn't say much. But, you know, she never does about these things. I suppose they're probably top secret."

"Top secret," Maya sighed pleasantly. "I would love to be a part of a top-secret mission."

"Yeah," Scarlett agreed, nodding so that her long platinum blonde hair swayed slightly. "Anyway, she said it wasn't a very big mission. There are only two of them going down to Earth this time."

"When's the mission?" Maya asked. Like "where," "when" was not a terribly uncommon question. The Land of the Clouds existed outside the flow of time. It was like a fern on the bank of a large river. Though the fern might get splashed by water sometimes, it wasn't a part of the river.

"Um . . ." Scarlett scratched her chin in thought. "I think my mom said 1400s CE. Whenever there were all those kings in Europe."

Maya sighed again as they passed a small office building. "I would love to time travel."

"We're learning how to in school. In just a few years—"

"I know, I know. But I'm ready now. I want to time travel. I know I could time travel." Her voice was yearning, betraying her obsessiveness. Her eyes glittered frighteningly.

"Maya," started Scarlett, raising her shield, preparing for an argument.

"Don't 'Maya' me! I'm ready!" Maya could feel the heat in her tone rising. "I'm the best in the class, and I want to get out of here!"

She began walking faster, leaving Scarlett in her wake. It was true. She knew she was the best in the class at the principles of time travel. So why wouldn't anyone let her do it? It isn't fair, she thought, practically screaming the words in her head.

Maya's cheeks were flushed with anger by the time she reached school. She wrenched open the door to her classroom, stomped to the back of the room, and sat down in her seat. Scarlett came in a few minutes later. She stared at Maya for a moment as if trying to read her mind, then took her own seat two rows away.

At 7:15, the bell rang for first period. It wasn't loud, just a faint buzz in the background.

The teacher, Sir Galiston, entered the room, sweeping his cloak as he did so. Tall and broad, he looked like a hero from one of Earth's medieval stories. Amused by Sir Galiston's entrance, Maya almost turned to roll her eyes at Scarlett before remembering that Scarlett was probably still mad at her.

"Good morning, class," Sir Galiston said. His voice was high pitched and squeaky, like that of a baby bird.

"Good morning, sir," responded the class in a dull fashion. Their lack of enthusiasm wasn't due to the fact that Sir Galiston's class was bad. More that he was often overdramatic. In fact, Sir Galiston was one of the best, most experienced teachers in all of the Land, having been on the front lines in one of the greatest battles of all time. He would regale them with stories most every day in his class, History of the Land. Today was no exception.

"Now," he announced in his strange chirp. "The next subject in your curriculum is the War of the OCT. Luckily for you, I fought in that war." He made a flourished bow, and half of the class, Maya included, smothered their giggles.

It was hard for Maya to stay angry and on edge when Sir Galiston told stories. He made them bright and fun, unlike the textbooks, which turned lively tales into dry dust. And as Sir Galiston began, Maya felt her anger receding like the tide. It was not gone, just removed from her focus for the time being.

"It must have been over a hundred years ago," Sir Galiston said, striding up and down the front of the room. "I was only a boy—well, I was seventeen. I had just discovered my power . . . Yes, seventeen," he repeated, seeing their looks of astonishment. "It was much more common to discover your power around age sixteen or so back then, not at twelve.

"Anyway, my power, as I'm sure you all know, is flight. Not a terribly uncommon power, but still . . . Now, who here actually knows what the OCT were?" Only a few students raised their hands, Scarlett among them. Maya supposed her mother had told her about them.

"Ah, well," mused Sir Galiston. "I should probably tell you about them, then. 'OCT' stands for the Organization to Control Time, and the Octagons were People of the Land of the Clouds, just like you. You kids all know how we try to interfere with human affairs as little as possible, right? Well, the OCT wanted to control time and the outcome of human events. That completely violated the Standard of Time Travel, which stated that we would use time travel only to keep humanity safe.

"They wore awful black robes with an octagon emblazoned on the back and always traveled in groups of eight. It was their lucky number." Some giggled, most likely at the notion that an evil organization could have a lucky number.

"No—don't laugh. The Octagons were dreadful people. Their motto was 'Beware the storm,'" Sir Galiston continued.

"Anyway, there were several skirmishes between them and the rest of us in the Land before the great battles began. Their leader, Fredrick von Hopsburg, had the power to transform his appearance and often appeared as a young boy. One skirmish began when he . . ."

And so Sir Galiston rambled on, describing the war in enthralling detail and also recounting his own brave actions that saved the mayor, leader of the Land. "Thus," he concluded, "we good People of the Land vanquished the OCT. However, I must tell you, they are still out there. They mostly reside on Earth now, hiding in the shadows, making mischief, interfering with human governments and history. Many of the Land's missions to Earth involve correcting their mistakes."

Maya saw many of her classmates cast a furtive glance at Scarlett, whose cheeks were now turning cherry red; the class knew about Scarlett's mother.

"There will undoubtedly be a time when the OCT attempts to regain its former might," Sir Galiston informed his pupils. "As you should know, after the war, Grenna the Great made the prophecy that is now engraved on the fountain in every town square across the Land of the Clouds."

Many students nodded at this. Most of them, Maya included, walked past the fountain every day.

"The prophecy goes, 'The child—'"

But at this point, the bell had hummed, and Sir Galiston dismissed the class, shouting after them in his squeaky voice that he would carry on with this story tomorrow.

Signals (Panasonic ZS200, Procreate, Lightroom)
Sage Millen 13
Vancouver, British Columbia, Canada

Highlights from Stonesoup.com

From Flash Contest #34

A River Flows in Me

By Inca Acrobat, 11
San Francisco, CA

You fail to speak to me
Even when the moon has risen
Above the glittering Loire
When my mind is awake
But my body still
Especially then

You turn your back away
My dreams fade away

About the Stone Soup Flash Contests

Stone Soup holds a flash contest during the first week of every month. The month's first Weekly Creativity prompt provides the contest challenge, and submissions are due within a week. Up to five winners are chosen for publication on our blog. The winners, along with up to five honorable mentions, are announced in the following Saturday newsletter. Find all the details at Stonesoup.com/post/stone-soup-monthly-flash-contest-winners-roll/.

Honor Roll

Welcome to the Stone Soup Honor Roll. Every month, we receive submissions from hundreds of kids from around the world. Unfortunately, we don't have space to publish all the great work we receive. We want to commend some of these talented writers and artists and encourage them to keep creating.

STORIES

Audrey Chang, 13
Dylan Ecimovic, 11
Sahara Muhammad, 12
Avery Parsons-Carswell, 10
Maayan Mardiks Rappaport, 10
Andrea Shi, 13
Hannah Slater, 9

POEMS

Priscilla Chow, 7
Chloe Garcia, 13
Sonia Kamnitzer, 9
Brooks Pinney, 10
Clarke Rodney, 10
Maya Ruben, 10

PERSONAL NARRATIVE

Carlos Ahearn, 11
Mariana Del Rio, 12
Noa Mehler, 11
Taia Reitz, 11
Clara Shore-Coloni, 11
Matthew Wang, 7

ART

Cleo Friedman, 9
Paris Andreou Hadjipavlou, 7
Lucas Hinds, 13
Aditi Nair, 13
Sophia Torres, 13
Jiacheng Yu, 6

Visit the Stone Soup Store at Stonesoupstore.com

At our store, you will find . . .

- Current and back issues of *Stone Soup*
- Our growing collection of books by young authors, as well as themed anthologies and the *Stone Soup Annual*
- High-quality prints from our collection of children's art
- Journals and sketchbooks

. . . and more!

Finally, don't forget to visit Stonesoup.com to browse our bonus materials. There you will find:

- More information about our writing workshops and book club
- Monthly flash contests and weekly creativity prompts
- Blog posts from our young bloggers on everything from sports to sewing
- Video interviews with *Stone Soup* authors

. . . and more content by young creators!

CPSIA information can be obtained
at www.ICGtesting.com
Printed in the USA
LVHW081605061121
702547LV00001B/1